Mark's Noble Quest

Rosaline's Curse

Book Two

Katharine Campbell

Special thanks to my sister, Dr. Anne-Marie Snoddy. Because of her careful review, I can assure my readers that absolutely everything in this book is scientifically accurate.

A Note On The Illustrations

A couple years ago one of my readers, Grace Woods, started sending me fan art. Seeing how she imagined my characters always made me smile. I was especially impressed with how she got their personalities to shine through just right. After beta-reading *Mark's Noble Quest*, she sent me fan art that made me laugh so hard I hired her to do the illustrations I've included in this book.

I hope you enjoy them as much as I did!

Katy Campbell

STOP!
Do not read this book until you've read Rosaline's Curse!

This novelette is a direct sequel to *Rosaline's Curse*. If you attempt to skip the first book and start with this one, you may find yourself, like Mark, confused, struggling, and lacking critical information. Unlike Mark, you won't persevere and come out stronger. Instead, if you come out at all, you will be frustrated and resentful.

Since I am not a fairy, I can't create a magical quest that will allow you to face and overcome such resentments. They will be stuck festering in your heart until you either snap, get a really good therapist, or get distracted and forget this book exists. So save yourself the emotional turmoil and just start with the first book.

Mark's Problem

Mark Reid had a problem. It wasn't just that he had been kicked out of university, or that his parents had disowned him, or even that he was in a foreign country hiding from a god-like being who wanted to murder him. It was, simply, that the woman he loved thought he was a wimp.

He first got this impression when he came to pick Rosaline up from work. She had a job mucking out stalls at a farm that offered trail rides to tourists. For a woman from the thirteenth century, it was an ideal position. Although animal husbandry had changed somewhat since her time, a pitchfork was still a pitchfork. In Rosaline's opinion, the best thing about the job was that she got to go riding for free.

When Mark pulled up outside the stables, he found her waiting there with two horses saddled and ready. One was a shiny light brown with a dark mane and tail, the other was dabbled-gray and comparatively chunky.

"Come on, Mark!" she called, as he stepped out of his car. "We're going riding!"

"Um, Ros..." Mark began. "You... you know I can't ride, right?"

"What?" she exclaimed.

"I've never even been on a horse," Mark explained. "I mean, when I was little I rode a horse at the carnival, but that hardly counts."

Rosaline's jaw dropped. "But... but you drive a car, don't you?"

"Exactly," Mark answered. "That's why I've never had to ride a horse."

"You don't need to learn to ride before you learn to drive?" Rosaline questioned.

"No," Mark answered. "It's a completely unrelated skillset." He separated his hands to illustrate.

"Oh," Rosaline realized. "Well, that's alright." She motioned to one of the waiting horses. "Come on, I'll teach you."

"Wait, *now?*" Mark blurted.

"It's very easy," Rosaline grinned. "Hop up!"

Mark's face paled a little. "The thing is... I wasn't expecting... I'm not..."

Rosaline raised an eyebrow as he sputtered excuses. After giving him a minute, she asked: "Are you afraid, Mark?"

"What? No," Mark answered as a bead of sweat slid down from his temple. "I'm just... not used to large animals."

He approached the brown horse.

"It's good though... I can... maybe..." He didn't know what he was saying or doing. All he knew was he didn't want to look like a *complete* fool. Maybe patting the horse on the nose would be enough to prove that to Rosaline? Only when he was right in front of the animal did he realize how tall it was. He placed a cautious hand on its muzzle.

It was very soft, like velvet. Perhaps horses were not as terrifying as he thou...

The horse snorted.

Mark jolted backward and Rosaline burst out laughing.

"It's not a lion, Mark!" she exclaimed. "It doesn't want to eat your hand!"

"Look, I'm just not used to them, alright?" Mark grumbled.

She doubled over, clutching her

stomach.

"You're afraid of horses," she breathed, trying to recover herself. "You're afraid of horses!"

She clutched her sides as she shook with laughter. The idea that a grown man could be afraid of horses was too much for her to bear.

Unfortunately, that incident was only the beginning of Mark's humiliation. A few days later, as he was walking with Rosaline through a crowded Lysandrian street, a young man whistled and said something in Kalathean that made Rosaline spin 'round on him in a rage.

Mark's Kalathean was still very rough but he knew both from the stranger's tone and body language that whatever he said was a catcall. Mark put his arm around Rosaline's shoulder defensively and tried to hurry her out of the situation.

But Rosaline slid out from under his protective arm.

"Are you going to let him speak to me like that?" she demanded.

"Ros," Mark mumbled, turning red and trying to lower his voice. "Let's just go, we don't want to cause–"

"He insulted my honor and you're just going to walk away?" Rosaline breathed in disbelief.

The catcaller was a tiny man whose freeflying curls were a physical manifestation of his carefree, playful personality. He was sitting on the steps of a thousand-year-old apartment building with a half-dozen ne'er-do-well companions.

When he heard them speaking together in English, he threw out his arms, grinned and approached Mark saying, "Come, we fight! We fight!"

Mark turned bright red, grabbed Rosaline's hand and made a hasty retreat through the crowd. The catcaller and his friends dissolved into laughter and yelled, "Run, tourist! The tourist runs!" Then they added the rudest words they knew in English.

Rosaline, however, knew something the catcaller didn't know: how to use rude English words correctly. She fired off a few salty insults as Mark dragged her away.

When they finally slowed to a walk, she hissed. "Those men would have lost their tongues for speaking to me like that in Kaltehafen."

"You're not in Kaltehafen," Mark reminded.

"No," Rosaline agreed, shooting Mark a little scowl. "A Kaltic man wouldn't walk away from someone who insulted his princess."

"Well maybe Kaltic men should learn that violence is not the solution to every problem," Mark grumbled.

Rosaline crossed her arms. "You could have fought him with words."

"Lovely," Mark replied. "I make him angry. He fights me, I defend myself, someone gets hurt, we get deported and Mr. King gets us both. Is that what you want?"

Rosaline frowned and folded her arms.

"No," she finally sighed before they resumed their walk to the bus stop in sulky silence.

"Sometimes," Mark continued. "It's best to just get out of a situation. Right?"

Rosaline shot him a look. In that look her thoughts were expressed plainly. She was a woman who had once been courted by warriors. In her mind, any man worth dating was a hero. What was Mark? An very ordinary, non-violent kind of twenty-first-century bloke. In other words, Mark was the kind of man Rosaline considered a coward.

A Fairy's Solution

"So, what you need to do is go to **Compose**," Mark explained. He was looking over the shoulder of an elderly monk at a computer screen.

Mark worked at Cedar Hill Monastery doing whatever Brother Joseph asked him to do. On good days, this was usually cataloging artifacts; and on days like today, it was showing Brother Nathan how to send emails.

"Here?" Brother Nathan asked.

"No, there," Mark explained. "Where it says **Compose**."

"Here?" the old man continued hovering the cursor over the **Spam Folder**.

"No, no," Mark continued patiently as he felt his life draining away. "*Here*. Where it says ***Compose***."

"Oh! Where it says **Compose**?" the old monk realized.

"*Yes*," Mark breathed, struggling to hold back tears of joy. "*That's it*."

He was so overwhelmed with relief that he didn't hear someone approaching from behind. When a cheery voice said, "Ready for morning tea?" Mark jumped three feet in the air.

"What the fffff..." Mark caught himself just in time. "...iddlesticks."

"Remind me not to have you teach anyone English," Brother Joseph smirked.

Mark turned a deep crimson.

"You can't sneak up on people like that," he whispered, eager to change the subject. "Brother Nathan's ninety-three: you'll give him a heart attack. And then you'll probably explode into sand because of that fairy rule."

"He's alright," Brother Joseph remarked. Then raising his voice a little he called, "Aren't you, Brother Nathan?"

Brother Nathan was still staring at the computer.

"What?" the old man yelled. "Who's that?" Then turning around, he said, "Oh! Brother Joseph!"

"See?" Brother Joseph grinned. "Brother Nathan is unshakable! Now come on, it's morning tea time!"

Brother Joseph didn't always have morning tea with Mark. There really wasn't any specific tea time in Kalathea, despite the nineteenth century British occupation. Yet, the old monk always managed to offer it when he noticed Mark was feeling down. And he *always* noticed when Mark was feeling down, no matter how hard the latter tried to hide it.

"You've been distracted all morning," Brother Joseph stated as he offered Mark a mug.

"No I haven't," Mark blurted.

Brother Joseph narrowed his eyes. That one look seemed to say, *Are you really trying to lie to a magical being that has at least three thousand years of experience reading the body language of puny mortals such as yourself?*

What the old monk said with his mouth was, "You don't have to tell me anything; but if you don't, I can't help you."

"Rosaline thinks I'm a coward," Mark spilled. He then proceeded to tell Brother Joseph about the incident with the catcaller, among others.

"Do you know that one of Rosaline's old suitors tried to impress her by bringing her the head of a *lion?*" Mark continued. "And now she's got... me! What have I ever done?"

"Let me see," Brother Joseph answered. "You risked your dreams, your freedom, and your life trying to help her. You stood up to King, knowing full well what he was..."

"But I've never..." Mark began. He trailed off, trying to figure out how to put his thoughts into words. Finally, his shoulders slumped, he stared at the ground and mumbled: "...fought anyone or killed anything."

Brother Joseph raised his eyebrows. "Good," he answered.

"I don't mean I *want* to kill something," Mark corrected quickly. "I've killed lab rats and that sort of thing..." He stared off into space as he recalled the memory, then mumbled: "That was really sad." Then, snapping himself to the present he continued, "In any case, I'm not condoning violence. I just want Rosaline to know that I am willing to fight for her. You know, if I *need* to."

"Are you?" Brother Joseph asked.

"Of course!" Mark exclaimed. "If there is any girl in the world worth fighting for, it's her! I just wish there was some 'mighty deed' I could do to prove it. Preferably one that doesn't involve hurting people or wildlife."

He sighed.

Brother Joseph sipped his tea thoughtfully. A moment passed in silence before he said, "Come to dinner tomorrow. And bring Rosaline."

———

Mark had the distinct impression that there was some specific reason Brother Joseph asked them to dinner. Yet, halfway through the meal, the fairy *still* hadn't brought up anything of any importance. He mostly asked Rosaline and Mark about what Kalathean tourist sites they had visited since their arrival.

"Have you explored up north at all?" Brother Joseph asked. "There are some lovely trails at the base of Mount Troma."

Mark and Rosaline shook their heads.

"I left a ring up there," Brother Joseph remembered.

Mark leaned forward in his chair. It was normally next to impossible to get Brother Joseph to talk about himself. Considering the monk was at least three thousand years old and part of an intelligent species Mark didn't even know existed until recently, this was torture to his scientific mind. Was the immortal really on the precipice of sharing a memory? Maybe, just maybe, a little of Mark's ravenous curiosity was about to be satisfied.

"The Fire Stone," Brother Joseph sighed. "A blood-red ruby set among silver and diamonds formed from the fires of Mount Troma—a symbol of endless devotion."

"And you lost it?" Rosaline accused.

"Oh no," Brother Joseph continued. "I left it up there on purpose... you see, I'm something of a romantic. I was hoping a noble knight would brave the mountain to retrieve the stone for his lady." The old monk sighed. "But... as of yet, no one has. And there aren't many knights around these days."

"We could get it in a helicopter," Rosaline suggested.

"Oh no!" Brother Joseph laughed. "Anyone can go to the top of the mountain in a helicopter, but only the man with a hero's heart can claim the stone."

Mark stiffened a little when Brother Joseph shot him a sly glance.

"To reach the stone," the monk continued, "an adventurer must undergo three trials designed to test his strength, virtue, and fortitude."

"Sounds downright Arthurian," Mark mumbled as he tapped his thumbs together nervously.

"Indeed!" the monk grinned. "It's extremely difficult. The Fire Stone is a symbol of love; and, like love, it requires struggle and sacrifice! In the end, its beauty makes all the work worthwhile."

Rosaline's eyes sparkled.

"I suppose it will be stuck on the mountain forever," Brother Joseph sighed. "Most men these days are too soft to even attempt such a quest. They like their tea and warm beds and hot showers and..." the old monk continued rambling, the glee in his tone increased slightly when he noticed Mark scowling at him.

"Oh look at the time!" Brother Joseph finally exclaimed. "You've both got work tomorrow! I'm so sorry!"

They wrapped up the conversation and started collecting their things. Mark lived in a beaten trailer on the monastery grounds, but he always insisted on seeing Rosaline home safely. He lingered behind a moment after she stepped through the door; then, turning to Brother Joseph he said, "I need a few days off."

Brother Joseph, looking exceptionally pleased with himself, answered, "I had a feeling you would say that."

Brother Joseph's Handy Gifts

"Are you sure you want to do this?" Brother Joseph asked. He was standing at a trail head beside Mark. Mount Troma loomed ominously in the distance. Mark had told Rosaline that he would be away for a few days running an errand for Brother Joseph.

"No," Mark answered. "But I'm going to."

"I can't tell you for sure what you'll face up there," Brother Joseph warned. "I... created the *program*, so to speak, but I can't say exactly how it will react to you."

Mark looked at him questioningly.

"I designed this quest to create trials based on what it finds in each adventurer's heart," the old monk elaborated. "And in that way, it forces you to face and defeat the evil within yourself."

"Oh," Mark answered, wondering whether or not this was a comforting revelation.

"The *good* news is," Brother Joseph grinned. "That if you run into some fire-breathing monster, it's just a physical manifestation of your character flaws, not endangered wildlife; so you should have no qualms at all about chopping it to bits."

"Chopping it to bits?" Mark questioned. "With what?"

"With this," Brother Joseph answered, thrusting a sword into Mark's arms.

"Where were you keeping *that?*" Mark exclaimed as he stumbled under the weight of the weapon.

"The same place I was keeping this," Brother Joseph said, stepping aside to reveal a gray and black horse, saddled and ready.

Mark's eyes widened. "That's not for me, right? I can't ride."

"Not to worry!" Brother Joseph grinned, patting the horse's nose. "Artemis here will do all the work for you. Just try not to fall off."

All the color was gone from Mark's face as he stared in horror at the animal. It was a magic horse, wasn't it? One that Brother Joseph created from mid-air for the specific purpose of taking him to the top of Mount Troma? If that was the case, he didn't have to worry about it biting him, or throwing him, or wandering off the trail to eat grass.

"Also, don't forget to feed her and brush her so she doesn't get saddle-sores," the old monk continued. "I put instructions in your saddlepack."

So it was a magic horse that he needed to care for... *that* would certainly add to the realism of this whole thing.

"How do I get on?" Mark asked.

"Hands on the saddle, left foot in the stirrup, pull yourself up and swing your leg over," Brother Joseph explained.

"Oh, is that all," Mark mumbled.

It took him six tries but he finally made it up. All the while, Artimis stood patiently reacting to his falls and exclamations only with the occasional judgmental glance. Her calm demeanor was a great comfort. She had to be some kind of illusion, because there was no way a real horse would ever be so calm under the circumstances.

"Please tell me that was the first trial," Mark asked when he finally settled into his seat.

"The trials don't start until you reach the mountain," Brother Joseph grinned. "Listen, I've packed a few extra things for you. Things I *guessed* might be useful."

Mark glanced over his shoulder at the pack on the back of his saddle.

"Then you must have some idea of what I'll face up there," Mark insisted.

"Oh I have ideas," Brother Joseph agreed. "I just can't say for certain. Now best of luck to you!"

"Wait!" Mark called, but the old monk vanished.

Mark clutched the reins and began grumbling to himself. Fairies, even the good ones, could be infuriating sometimes.

Artemis started walking toward the mountain unprompted and it was then that Mark realized he hadn't asked Brother Joseph how to get down. He reached into his pocket for his mobile with one hand, while clutching the reins with the other. Of course, he didn't have any data so there was no way he could Google it. He did have some cellular reception though.

He called Rosaline but got her voicemail. She was probably still working.

"Um, hi, Ros," he started when he heard the beep. "I have a somewhat urgent question– nothing to worry about though!" He added the last sentence quickly, not wanting her to panic. "But if it's not too much trouble, can you call me back? Sooner rather than later, preferably. Um… thanks. Alright. I love you. Bye."

There wasn't much more he could do for the moment; luckily, he wouldn't have to think about dismounting for a while. How hard could it be?

After a little time riding, he realized he was starting to enjoy himself. He had gotten used to the height, it was a nice day, and the landscape was pretty. Hills rolled away in all directions, dotted with shrubs and short trees. The mountain rising up over the rolling hills was a breathtaking spectacle.

Mark had spent most of the previous evening researching Mount Troma. It was a volcano. The last eruption happened a hundred years ago, and the next one wasn't due to occur for a while. Hopefully not until long after Mark was finished with his quest.

By the end of the day, he had made it a little ways up the mountain and hadn't encountered any kind of trial. Rosaline hadn't returned his call, so he dismounted by slipping off the horse sideways and landing on his scabbard.

As he stood up, rubbing the bruise on his hip, he was grateful Rosaline hadn't seen. He would never have heard the end of it.

He took the saddlepack down from his horse and began to look through the things Brother Joseph packed. Sitting right on the top of the contents was a little packet of ear plugs. Mark furrowed his brow. He was alone, in the wilderness, facing he didn't know what. Why in the *world* would he want to plug his ears?

He shrugged, set the earplugs aside, and looked back in the pack to see the Styrofoam corner of some kind of container. He grabbed this as best he could and pulled. It was awkward and kept slipping out of his grip, but he slowly wriggled it loose. The thing seemed to grow as he struggled to pull it out of the leather saddle pack. At last, he flipped the bag upside down and out slid a full-sized foam cooler. He blinked.

He looked at the saddlepack, then back at the cooler. Clearly, there was some magic involved here because the cooler was at least twice the size of the pack. Mark found a Sticky Note on the lid that read:

For the dragon's head.
- Brother Joseph

Mark cracked the cooler open, releasing a bluish mist. Was this more magic? Upon examination, he found that the bluish mist was only the product of perfectly normal, non-magic, dry ice.

Could this really be for transporting the decapitated head of some monster? That would mean he'd have to fight a monster... and then *win* said fight. Mark decided to set the cooler aside and think about something else for a while.

He found two other items at the bottom of the saddlepack: a USB charging stick and a wallet-sized photograph.

"Just like the knights of old," Mark chuckled, as he held up the charging stick. He set it aside and looked at the printed photo. It was one he took of Rosaline while they were on their way back from the *Lysandrian Museum of History.*

Normally, Rosaline carefully posed every time she noticed Mark holding up his mobile. But on that day, a combination of speed and stealth produced a natural portrait of her laughing as her curls bounced freely around her face.

The second Rosaline realized what he had done, she started fighting him for his device, giggling "Delete that!" as he pulled it out of her reach.

"I don't think I will," Mark grinned. "In fact, look at this!" He turned his mobile screen toward her. "It's my background now!"

Mark loved that photo; not only because it captured Rosaline's personality perfectly, but because it reminded him of one of their happiest days together. Just the two of them mucking around in the history museum, sharing knowledge, flirting, and hoping no one would recognise them as infamous skeleton thieves and throw them out.

Mark flipped the photograph over. Scrawled on the back were the words:

Remember what you're fighting for.
- Brother Joseph

The First Trial: A Test of Strength

Though Mark was somewhat new to mythical quests, he was not new to backpacking. As such, he owned some basic camping supplies and had the foresight to bring them along. When the sunlight began to dim, he set-up his tent, ate a freeze dried substance labeled *chicken*, and took care of Artemis according to the instructions Brother Joseph provided. At this point, he had made it to the foot of the mountain so he thought a good night of sleep would be a prudent way to prepare for whatever horrors awaited him toward the summit.

Unfortunately, sometime in the middle of the night, his sleep was interrupted by a distant voice.

"Mark? Is that you in there?"

A chill ran down Mark's spine as the eerie sound broke into his consciousness. He opened his eyes to find himself bundled up inside his tent. It was still dark, he could hear insects chirping outside the canvas walls. He sat up blinking as his tired mind struggled to process the sound coming from outside.

"Mark, I need you," the voice commanded. "*At once.*"

He stiffened. If he didn't know better, he'd say it was his mother's voice. But what would his mother be doing standing around in the

Kalathean countryside, in the middle of the night? Besides, there was something off about that voice. It was unnatural somehow, distant... *hollow*.

A strange blue light illuminated the inside of his tent. At first, Mark assumed this was moonlight, but when he finally found his glasses and got a look at the source, he stiffened in horror. The glow was coming from a human figure standing just outside the door.

Mark gripped the hilt of his sword and shimmied from his sleeping bag toward the anomaly. He unzipped the exit just enough to peer through... then immediately zipped it back up. *It was a ghost*. And she'd been looking right at him.

"Out, Mark!" the woman ordered. "If any of my servants behaved this way, I'd cut their heads off. Don't think for a moment you can get away with ignoring me because you're my descendant."

Mark's mind rushed to make sense of the apparition. If it wasn't for the fact that the ghost was blue, translucent, and dressed like some ancient noblewoman, Mark would have thought it was his mother. She had the same strong jaw and the same hard, cutting eyes. She stood with her head up and her shoulders back like she was the self-appointed ruler of the world.

"There's no sense hiding, Mark," the voice continued. "I know you're in there."

She had a point. Now that she'd seen him, he might as well stop cowering behind a sliver of cloth. He slowly unzipped the tent and, gripping his sword in one hand, crawled out and rose to his feet. A sword probably wasn't much use against a ghost, but it couldn't possibly hurt to bring it along.

The woman regarded him with reproving eyes. Mark's stomach twisted. He had been here before. Well not exactly *here*, per se, but under the reproachful gaze of a practically identical woman.

This had to be one of the trials, right? Brother Joseph had said that each of the trials were created from something in the adventurer's heart. Therefore, this ghostly queen was a projection of something in his subconscious. That would explain not only why she looked just like his mother, but why, despite her outdated sense of fashion, she spoke modern English.

Mark trembled as her gaze moved from his head to his feet and back up again.

"Weak," the noblewoman declared. "Puny... and trembling all over." She shook her head disapprovingly. "I expected more from Margaret's son. Though I don't know why. So far, she's the only one of my descendants that hasn't been a *complete* disappointment."

Mark's mouth fell open. "Um, sorr–," he started.

But she interrupted him with a wave of her hand. "Doesn't matter, as of right now you happen to be the descendant I need. Come on."

She turned, motioning for him to follow.

Mark remained rooted to the spot. He had seen enough of his flatmate's horror films to know that following a ghost into the desert was probably a bad idea.

She looked over her shoulder at him and scowled. "Well, don't stand there gaping! You've got work to do!"

"Look, Mum, I–" Mark started.

The ghost turned on him with the force of a hurricane.

"Let me make something *clear*," she stated. "I am *not* your mother. If it weren't for the sacrifices I made in the tenth century, your mother would never have *existed* in the twentieth."

"Oh," Mark breathed.

"I am Lady Eadburg. You may address me as Your Ladyship. Is that clear?"

"Yes, Mum," Mark replied. "I mean, Your Ladyship."

"Now, come!" she ordered.

Mark remained rooted to the spot.

"I mean no disrespect, Your Ladyship," he started. "But, um, what's all this about?"

Her scowl deepened. Her gaze cut into him.

"What an awful generation," she sighed. "Disrespectful, insolent, questioning nobility like it's nothing at all. As if *my* people hadn't struggled and suffered and fought for *your* future."

"Sorry," Mark breathed. "I just... need to know what it is you want me to do."

"I've gone to pieces, Mark," she explained. "And I need you to put me back together."

Mark blinked. Aside from the fact that she was clearly a ghost, nothing about her gave him the impression she had gone to pieces. In fact, his mother was firmly against the idea of anyone ever going to pieces. Whenever it happened to one of her employees, she would say,

"If you can't handle stress, you shouldn't be in the finance department!"

He tried to remind himself that this ghost was *not* his mother. While his mother was a bit ruthless, she'd probably never had anyone's head cut off. This tenth-century noblewoman clearly *had*... meaning it was in Mark's best interest to keep her happy.

"Um, sorry," Mark started. "You want me to... put you back together?"

"My skeleton," the noblewoman explained. She rolled her eyes as if she couldn't believe she actually needed to clarify this. "It got all mixed up in the last eruption."

"So you need me to excavate your skeleton?" Mark questioned.

"And put it back together," Lady Eadburg explained. "So my spirit can find peace."

Mark's eyes brightened. *Was this his first trial?* He was born for this!

After getting kicked out of university, he never imagined ever doing any kind of an excavation ever again. How was this a trial? It was as if Brother Joseph had sworn to torture him and then sent him to an amusement park instead.

Of course, the excavation would probably be difficult since he didn't have any of the proper equipment... but that would depend on soil conditions and such.

"Oh, yeah, I can help with that," Mark smiled.

Then he proceeded to do exactly the thing he'd sworn not to do a few moments prior: he followed a ghost into the wilderness.

"I bet you're wondering how an Anglo-Saxon noblewoman ended up scattered across the Kalathean desert," Lady Eadburg grumbled.

"I just assumed it had something to do with fairy magic and um, my subconscious," Mark added.

"Wrong! Wrong!" Lady Eadburg replied, aggressively shaking her head. "You won't believe it when I tell you, Mark! In 1908, these two Kalathean hooligans stole me out of England along with six tea kettles."

Mark raised his eyebrows. "Six tea kettles?"

"I know, it's beyond me!" she exclaimed. "Walking into someone else's country and taking artifacts without permission is the very *definition* of unacceptable behavior! Someone ought to civilize these people." She shook her head disapprovingly. "And if THAT wasn't bad enough, they abandoned me at the base of Mount Troma. That's inexcusable, even if they *were* fleeing an eruption."

They came to the top of a shrubby hill, and Mark looked down to see a wide, flat, expanse carpeted in reddish sand. Lady Eadburg continued ranting as they walked.

"After everything I've done, no one remembers who I was or where I am. It's unacceptable, to say the least."

Mark nodded along as she spoke. She wasn't the easiest person to get along with, but he did feel sorry for her. And he was her descendant afterall; if anyone owed her respect, it was him.

They continued down into this expanse; and when Mark stepped into the area, he felt the sand squish down beneath his shoes. It seemed to be loose, at least on the surface. Mark's feet left indentations as he crossed the area. He glanced sideways at Lady Eadburg, noticing how her feet left no impressions at all. This was completely expected but still unsettling.

Her Ladyship eventually stopped and extended her slender arm toward the ground at her feet.

"Here," she stated.

Mark looked carefully at the area; but, seeing nothing, he knelt down and began sifting through the sand with his hands. By now, the horizon was starting to brighten. That, along with Lady Eadburg's glow, gave him a reasonable amount of light.

After only a few moments, he found what appeared to be a metatarsal floating in the loose sand. He continued sifting, withdrawing a tibia fragment, calcaneus, and for some reason an ethmoid. Her ladyship wasn't lying when she said she'd gone to pieces—her head and her feet were all mixed up.

Mark continued working, all the while wondering how this was supposed to be a trial. It was the easiest excavation he'd ever been on.

When he was a boy, his nanny buried a bunch of plastic dinosaurs in the sand pit for him. Even *that* excavation was harder than this one.

As Mark worked, Her Ladyship took a seat on a rock a short distance away and watched, her hands folded gracefully on her lap.

Whenever he withdrew a bone from the sand, he grouped it with bones of similar type to make reassembly easier.

"You're well suited to this," Lady Eadburg complimented after a time.

Her Ladyship probably thought crawling around in the dirt at her feet was the ideal occupation for the majority of people. Still, Mark thanked her.

"You're methodical, at least," she continued. "Margaret was right to have you educated in the sciences. Pity you threw all that away."

Mark chomped down on his lower lip. Until this point, he'd been completely in his element. The act of digging up, organizing, and assembling bones had brought him such satisfaction that he'd forgotten the fact that once he'd completed this strange magical trial, he'd likely never work on any kind of an excavation ever again.

"Margaret's problem is that she only ever had one child," Her Ladyship continued. "I had fourteen! Seven survived to adulthood; and of those seven, only two were worth anything."

Mark had to take a moment to process this. "Um…" he mumbled. "I'm so sorry."

"If Margaret's line dwindles back into obscurity, she'll have no one to blame but herself," Eaburg paused, probably to shake her head. Mark's eyes were focused on the sand he was presently sifting. "Let this be a lesson to you, Mark. Never put all your hopes in one child!"

Mark made no reply at all. Her words had thrust him deep into a long-festering resentment.

Shortly after confessing his crimes to the authorities, he'd video-called his parents to tell them what he'd done. He knew they'd be angry, what parents wouldn't be?

At first, they didn't believe him. They thought maybe his confession was a joke of some kind. Once he assured them it wasn't, they decided someone at university must have misled him somehow. His mum and dad argued back and forth for a while about how to take legal action before Mark was finally able to break in and convince them that he had been acting of his own free will.

"How could you *do* this to us, Mark?" his mother had cried, before going on to remind him of every sacrifice she had ever made for him.

Sometimes Mark wondered if his parents really wanted a child at all, or if a child was just the only way they could think of to immortalize their own legacy. Every award Mark ever won from primary school through university was put in a place of honor in their house. His mum constantly boasted about his success to her friends.

As a child, she had him believing that any bad mark would condemn him to a life of poverty and crime. Ironically, Mark had been a star student his whole life and still ended up a criminal.

If Mark's mother had been any younger than sixty-three, she'd probably have taken a page out of Lady Eadburg's book: written Mark off as a loss and tried again with a new child.

He continued working for several hours, trying his best to tune out Lady Eadburg's unceasing opinions. Occasionally, he would nod and say something like, "I see," just to keep the ghost placated.

"I think I'm almost done," he said after a while.

"You found them all?" Lady Eadburg questioned. "All... how many bones does a skeleton have?"

"Usually adults have two hundred and six," Mark started. "But–"

"So you've found all two hundred and six then?" Lady Eadburg pressed.

"Well, after more than a thousand years, a trip across Europe, and a volcanic eruption, I doubt you have that many anymore," Mark shrugged.

"Then how are you to know when you've found them all?" she asked.

"I can't," Mark shrugged. "But my best guess is—"

"*Unacceptable,*" Lady Eadburg interrupted. "I don't want to hear anything about being finished until you've found all two hundred and six."

Mark stared at her.

"Look, Your Ladyship," he finally said. "You might not even have had that many in life! And even if you did, and by some miracle, they'd all survived this long, some of them are much too small for me to find–"

"If you weren't part of such an ungrateful generation," Lady Eadburg continued. "You'd have some respect for the remains of your forebears and see that they were all properly entombed."

"Do I really need *all two-hundred six* to bring your spirit peace?" Mark asked, the color draining from his face.

"Didn't I just say so?" Lady Eadburg scowled.

All of a sudden, this excavation felt more like an actual trial. Mark's mind raced. He didn't even have a magnifying glass, and the expanse of volcanic sand was vast.

"I need to make a call," he said finally. "Will you excuse me?"

"What, you're just going to walk away from me?" Lady Eadburg raised an eyebrow in disbelief.

"If you want me to help you," Mark explained. "I need to get some advice."

The lady scowled and sat back down on her rock. "Do what you must."

Mark pulled his mobile out of his pocket and jogged a short distance away. Once he was out of earshot, he dialed Brother Joseph.

"Are you stuck already?" came the monk's cheery voice.

Mark explained the situation as quickly as he could.

"She wants me to do the impossible," he whispered. "That can't be the only way to break her curse?"

"Are you sure there is a curse?" Brother Joseph asked.

"That's what she said," Mark continued. "She needs me to do this so her spirit can find peace."

"I see," Brother Joseph answered. "Well, Mark, from the sound of it, I don't think *you* can do anything to bring her spirit peace."

"What do you mean?" Mark spluttered. "That's the trial, isn't it?"

"I doubt it," Brother Joseph clarified. "If she wants to find peace, she needs to accept her own mortality."

"Oh," Mark stated, shooting a nervous look at the glowing figure over his shoulder. "She doesn't seem to realize that… should I tell her?"

"You can try."

"And then what?" Mark pressed.

"Just be as honest and as clear as you can, then continue your quest."

"So… I really can't do anything for her?" Mark questioned. "She is my ancestor after all."

Brother Joseph turned the question back on Mark: "What do *you* think?"

"I suppose…" Mark continued. "Assuming all this is real and not just some hallucination, I can report the bones to the proper authorities. They'll see they are treated respectfully."

"Perfect," Brother Joseph affirmed.

"She isn't going to like that," Mark objected.

"She isn't going to like anything you say," Joseph asserted. "What she wants is impossible. I'm afraid the only thing you can do is set a clear boundary and walk away."

Mark went silent for a moment before blurting, "What?"

"You can't solve her problem," the old monk repeated. "And you've got to be back by Saturday so you don't miss community service."

With the quest on Mark's mind, he'd almost forgotten about his community service hours. He sighed and rubbed his forehead. *Why had he broken so many laws?*

"But she's a ghost!" Mark pressed. "What if she–"

"What if she what?" Brother Joseph interrupted. "Complains?"

"I was thinking more like…comes into my tent, makes creepy noises, and knocks things over."

"What if she does?"

Mark was silent. The monk had a point. Could ghosts really do anything other than scare people? In some of John Paul's horror films they could, but this one didn't seem like that kind of ghost.

"So she can't hurt me?" Mark pressed.

"Probably not," Brother Joseph seemed to shrug.

Mark spent a moment, contemplating the "probably."

"Well, if I can't do anything for her…" he thought aloud. "Then what's the first trial?"

"Be clear, set your boundary, *and* stick to it."

"Yes, you said that," Mark insisted, frustration bubbling in his chest. "But I still don't understand what the first trial is."

There was a short silence before Brother Joseph said, "You'll figure it out."

Mark's throbbing head felt like it was going to pop. He sensed that the old monk was about to hang up.

"Just a moment!" he jumped in. "I've got one more question."

"Yes?"

"All of this… it's all from my subconscious, right?" he pleaded. "Nothing in these trials can actually hurt me, right?"

"Mark, the evil in your heart is very real," Brother Joseph warned, "and it can definitely hurt you."

"You mean spiritually, yeah? Or metaphorically?"

"Or physically," Brother Joseph clarified. "All the more reason to face and defeat it. Good luck!"

The monk hung up.

Mark stood for a long moment, clutching his phone, breathing deeply. So the trials were dangerous, but Brother Joseph didn't seem to think Lady Eadburg was…

One thing at a time, Mark, he thought before heading back in her direction.

She jumped up as she saw him approaching.

"Look, Your Ladyship," Mark started. "I've got some bad news."

Lady Eadburg folded her arms.

"Yes?" she demanded.

"So, I've just consulted an expert and the thing is..."

Her icy gaze drilled through him, sending a chill down his spine. It was silly for Mark to worry. A ghost couldn't remove the head of a physical person... *probably*.

"I can't solve your problem," Mark shrugged.

"What do you mean?"

Mark stiffened. Those simple words cut into him.

"Finding all your bones isn't going to bring you peace," Mark explained. "Nothing I can do will bring you peace. That's something you've got to work out yourself."

"Stop talking nonsense and resume your search, Mark," Lady Eadburg insisted.

"Look, that won't work," Mark tried to explain. "The only way for you to find peace is by accepting your mortality."

"Who is this *expert*?" Lady Eadburg demanded.

"Brother Joseph Sharma," Mark said. He held out his mobile. "You want to talk to him?"

"No," she answered, waving away the device. "I want you to stop talking to random clergymen and do your job."

"Look," Mark sighed. "I've done everything I can. I don't have the equipment or the time to keep looking; and even if I did, it wouldn't help you. I'm sorry."

"What do you mean, you don't have the time?" Lady Eadburg protested. "I am the reason you exist. You wouldn't have any time at all if it wasn't for me."

Mark felt the energy draining from his body. He'd been up since before dawn, digging around in the sand. He still had a long road ahead, and he desperately needed a little sleep. He had a feeling no amount of rationalizing would convince the ghost that she was asking the impossible.

"I'm sorry," Mark said. "This is all I can do."

He turned to go.

"Wait, Mark!" her tone was different now—soft, cracked. "I don't want to be forgotten."

A thorn of sympathy pierced his heart. He turned back around.

"Oh, Mu– Your Ladyship," Mark sighed. "You think I'm not grateful? If there was some way I could bring you peace, I would. But it's beyond my abilities!"

"It wouldn't be if you only tried!" she begged. "Five minutes more! You can at least give me that much, can't you?"

Mark considered this for a moment. She was his ancestor, and as such, he did owe her a great debt. That said, he knew that once the allotted five minutes expired, she'd ask for five more... and it would go on and on. It was also true that, while he owed his ancestors respect, he did not *belong* to them. He had his own responsibilities. The last thing he needed was to get thrown into prison for neglecting his community service hours.

He straightened up, breathed deeply and said, "Good night, Your Ladyship."

Technically, it was the afternoon; but given the fact he was falling asleep on his feet, "Goodnight," seemed the appropriate response.

She followed him back to his tent, all the while talking about how ungrateful he was and explaining to him, in detail, every sacrifice she'd ever made that had in some distant way led to his existence.

He lay down in his tent and closed his eyes, but her voice trailed on from somewhere in the air around him. Nagging him, keeping him awake, saying he was lazy and if he didn't get up, he'd continue to be a failure all his life.

Mark tossed and turned. It was as Brother Joseph said, the worst she could do was complain—unfortunately, she was very good at it. The longer Mark lay there beneath the endless torrent of her voice, the more resentful and guilty he felt.

Even though he couldn't see her, she was there, in his ears, in his mind, nagging at him, tearing him down, making him feel like a good-for-nothing, ungrateful, waste of space.

Set a clear boundary and stick to it. That was easy for Brother Joseph to say. If only there was some way he could block out the noise…

Mark sat bolt upright. At once, he went outside to Artemis's saddle pack and found the earplugs Brother Joseph had supplied. Lady Eadburg, of course, had been waiting outside the tent and was glaring at him as she continued to make her opinions known.

However, when she saw the earplugs in his hand, she went silent and looked up at him, her face full of hurt.

"Are you... are you really going to block me out, Mark?" she asked.

Mark suddenly felt like he'd been stabbed in the gut. Was he really going to block out his own mother? What kind of a monster was he?

She's not your mother, he repeated to himself over and over again. *She's probably not even real.* Unfortunately, the guilt he felt was very real. He met her gaze and said, "I won't if you'll just... accept what I told you."

She thrust her hands on her hips. "Accept that you're neglecting me?"

Mark popped the earplugs in and returned to his tent. Shortly thereafter, he was enjoying a much needed sleep.

The Second Trial: A Test of Virtue

Considering the fact that his tent was now haunted, Mark was in good spirits. He resumed his journey early the next morning after feeding Artemis with some oats he found in Brother Joseph's bottomless saddlepack.

He managed to ignore his angry ghost companion all night long. While he couldn't say for *sure* that was the solution to the first trial, it definitely took heroic effort on his part. Making it up on horseback in one try also added to his confidence; maybe he could be the hero Rosaline deserved after all?

After several pleasant hours of riding, Mark noticed a figure a ways up the mountainside ahead. He thought at first it was a hiker, but coming closer he noticed the person was standing next to some kind of giant horizontal cylinder on stilts.

Mark kept his gaze on this as he approached, trying to figure out what it was—a water tank maybe? As he came closer he realized it was some kind of engine. He was so busy wondering about it, he didn't get a good look at the person working on it until he was right up close.

When he did see her, his cheeks went crimson and his jaw dropped.

It was Alexa Brown.

When Alexa first appeared at King's gala wearing that tiny scarlet dress, Mark thought she was absolutely breathtaking. Now she was dressed in a plaid button up with pens in the breast pocket and chemical stained jeans. Her hair was tossed back in a pony tail and her eyes were partially concealed by giant thick-rimmed glasses. She was holding a multitool and her slender hands were smeared with engine grease.

Mark didn't think anything could trump the beauty from the gala, but this new Alexa was his own personal Venus. (Actually, she looked exactly like the dream girl he'd doodled in his notebook when he was fifteen.)

"Mark Reid!" she cried, suddenly looking up from the engine. "Is that you?"

He suddenly became very self conscious. The sword and the horse probably made him look like a nerd. She didn't seem to mind though.

Still, he thought it was best to dismount. The result of this decision was that he ended up sideways on the ground with a bruised hip.

"Are you alright?" Alexa asked.

Mark stood up and brushed himself off, collecting his dignity.

"Perfect," he answered.

"Oh good," she giggled.

Funny, he didn't remember Alexa being so giggly. Also, why was she so happy to see him? The last time he saw her, she had shot him a contemptuous look before storming out of his flat.

"So..." she shrugged. "What are you doing here, Mark?"

"Stuff and things," Mark blurted. "Um, what are you doing here?"

She giggled a little at his awkwardness, then adjusted her glasses and said, "Altitude testing."

"All on your own?" he asked.

She nodded, as if going alone to the top of a volcano in a foreign country to run altitude tests was a completely normal procedure.

An awkward silence passed.

"Um, listen, Alexa," Mark started. "I should probably apologize for–"

She held up a hand to stop him.

"Don't," she said. "I should have given you time to explain, instead of running off..."

Her cheeks flushed. Another awkward silence passed while they both stared at the ground.

When she finally managed to lock eyes with him, she grinned and said, "I had fun, you know."

"Yeah?" Mark asked, brightening. He couldn't actually remember much of what happened the last time they were together. He wished he could, it must have been wonderful.

He squinted a little as he tried to see her sparkling blue eyes through the deep lens that veiled them. Then his gaze wandered down to her lips. He remembered kissing those lips. That *was* wonderful.

His gaze might have made its way slowly down to her feet and then back up again except that he remembered something else that stopped him dead in his tracks—Rosaline's tears.

He winced as the recollection pierced his heart. How could he have been so stupid that night? *He was supposed to be helping her.* If he had stayed sober and focused, maybe Rosaline wouldn't have run away.

And if he had kept Rosaline's trust, he could have talked her out of stealing the bones. They could have found some other way of escaping Mr. King. Maybe they'd both still be in Wellingford with clean criminal records and he'd still be in university.

Rosaline was right, he was a coward. Because everything he did after leaving her that night, he did to drown out his own terror. He had used Alexa as a distraction from his fear of King, a fear he'd abandoned Rosaline to face on her own.

"I'd like to see you again," Alexa's voice snapped him from his thoughts.

She wanted to see him again? His heart began pounding. His dream girl wanted to see him again?

She'd probably never make him go on holy quests to steal relics, never make him climb a volcano to prove his manhood. Choosing Alexa meant, perhaps, he could go back to his old life.

But Mark hesitated again. The thing was... *he didn't want to be his old self.*

He wanted to be brave like Rosaline. Brave enough to face a world unknown, brave enough to strangle a sphynx, brave enough to trade his life for hers. He wanted to be curious *like her*, adventurous *like her*.

Alexa was lovely, but to Mark Reid, no woman in the world could compare to Rosaline.

"The thing is," Mark continued as he regarded Alexa with a furrowed brow. "The *real* Alexa doesn't want anything to do with me. She thinks I'm a cad and she's absolutely right."

"What are you talking about?" Alexa giggled.

"I don't suppose I'll ever see the real Alexa again," Mark sighed. "So, I'll say this to you instead."

Alexa was furrowing her brow now, while trying to maintain a stiff smile.

"I put you in such an awkward place that day," Mark blushed. "And I'm sorry. You didn't deserve that."

Alexa waved off his apology. "I've completely forgotten. Come on, Mark! Let's sit down over there and talk about something else."

Mark decided to respond in the way he wished he'd responded to the real Alexa when she'd asked him out for drinks during the gala.

"Thank you, but I'm sorry. I've already got plans."

He turned to go.

"So is that how it is?"

Something in Alexa's giggly voice had changed. It was cold and venomous. Mark spun around in time to see the hue of her skin changing to green. Her hair began to morph together into thicker strands with bulbous ends. The bulbs split open revealing fangs and flickering forked tongues. The glasses fell off and the plaid button-up morphed into a Grecian breastplate.

Mark tore his gaze away just in time. Venus was turning into Medusa, and Mark knew enough mythology to keep his eyes off her face. He did the thing any sensible man would do when the girl he just rejected morphs into a mythological beast– *he ran.*

Part of him felt like he should have seen this coming. Afterall, he realized that Alexa was an imposter from his subconscious around the same time he realized she was really, *really* into him. Still, he didn't think the imposter would take rejection *this* hard.

He glanced over his shoulder, careful to keep his eyes low so he would only see her feet and not her face. She was coming after him. Her scaly hand was visible out of the corner of his eye, holding some kind of a cleaver.

She was armed. This wasn't good. Mark was technically armed too, but he'd never fought anything in his life. Why hadn't the old monk given him a gun? He had no idea how to use a sword, especially when he couldn't look at his opponent.

He couldn't even use his shield as a mirror because *Brother Joseph hadn't given him a shield.* His mind raced as he continued running, his heart hammering in his chest.

Mark considered his options while trying to ignore the hisses and growls coming from behind him. *What did he have?* He whipped his mobile out of his pocket, turned on the camera app, flipped it into selfie mode, and used it to look over his shoulder. She was… way too close for comfort.

He scrambled up the rocky hillside with a dexterity he didn't know he possessed, while his mind raced for solutions. Okay, he could use the camera app to look at her, now what? She still had that bloody cleaver. There was no way he could beat this creature in hand-to-hand combat. *She* actually knew how to use her weapon.

What did he know that she didn't? He continued running in a big circle around the area where they had been talking, trying to buy time. He could see his horse standing at a distance ahead, completely unphased by the appearance of the mythological beast chasing him. Was that engine thing still where Alexa left it? Maybe he could blow it up?

He looked around for it but it must have vanished when Alexa transformed—just his luck. Then something else occurred to him—*he had dry ice.*

There are benefits and drawbacks to rooming with a chemistry student. One of the drawbacks is that chemistry students love blowing things up, and when you're renting, that can get you into trouble. One of the benefits is that if you are ever being chased by Medusa, you might remember how to blow stuff up yourself.

Mark drew his sword and raised it as he approached Artemis. He slid around her, slicing his saddle pack in half. Bluish mist and styrofoam exploded everywhere. Artemis shifted her feet a little but otherwise remained still. *Thank God, she wasn't a real horse.*

Mark scooped a handful of misty white pellets off the ground– and then swore loudly and dropped them. Running for his life had made him forget something about dry ice: it burned.

He glanced behind him, keeping his gaze low. She hadn't caught up with him yet, but she was on her way. He had seconds.

He snatched his water bottle off his backpack and popped the lid off. Then, bracing himself, he snatched a handful of dry ice and dropped it into the bottle. He repeated this, chomping down on his lips as the pellets seared his skin.

She was right on top of him now. He popped the lid back on his water bottle, pressed it down tightly, then ran. He needed to let the pressure build for a couple minutes. He tried to sheath his sword but missed, and ended up with the weapon dangling awkwardly between his belt and his waist with no time to correct the issue.

Pulling his mobile out of his pocket, he turned to face his nemesis. If he was just looking at pixels, it hardly mattered if he was in selfie mode or not. He would be alright as long as he didn't accidentally glance over the screen... probably. Just as she was raising her blade, he threw the bottle. As the bottom of the bomb met her forehead, the cap blew off and hit Mark's phone, knocking it away from his face.

If it hadn't been for the cloud of mist erupting between them, he probably would have been turned to stone. Mark had just enough time to snatch his device before he heard an angry roar and dodged a cleaver blow.

The bomb had succeeded in... denting his mobile and making the monster angry. *Brilliant.*

Fortunately, Medusa couldn't run as fast as Mark. Unfortunately, she didn't seem to be getting tired or short of breath, and Mark definitely was.

He needed to end this. The only good thing that came from Mark's little bomb experiment was that it taught him dry ice really, really hurt.

He swerved back toward the exploded cooler and grabbed a fistfull of styrofoam and dry ice pellets.

His eyes watered as it burned into his skin. He held his phone in front of his face with one hand and clung to the ice with the other. His cheeks were red, his fist was shaking in pain, his eyes watered, but he didn't let go.

She was almost close enough... a few more seconds. She raised her cleaver and Mark leapt forward, flinging the pellets in her eyes. She screamed and crumpled over covering her face with her hands. Mark dropped his mobile, drew his weapon, and brought it down on the back of her neck with both hands.

He didn't watch the head fall as he didn't want to risk seeing the face if it rolled. Instead, he kept his eyes up until the hissing of the snake hair ceased. Then he removed his jacket and threw it over the lifeless ball.

The sight of the lump under his jacket made Mark explode into a fit of laughing, crying, and shaking. He was alive! Not only that, he'd killed Medusa! What would Rosaline say when he showed her the head? Probably nothing, because if she saw it, she'd turn to stone. He lay down onto the ground and curled into the fetal position, laughing like a maniac. Maybe he'd just let her see a bit of the top.

As the adrenaline wore off, he realized that his hand was in agony. He examined his scarlet palm and then released a naughty exclamation that rang out through the valley. It was not "fiddlesticks".

The Third Trial: A Test of Fortitude

The idea of **not** entering the spooky cave on the summit occurred to Mark, but he quickly dismissed it. First of all, the yawning cavern looked like exactly the sort of place a cheeky fairy would hide a ring. Second, even if the ring wasn't there, how could he not take a quick look? At the very least, the cave probably contained some interesting rock formations or bats or something.

He left Artemis outside and proceeded cautiously, holding his torchlight awkwardly in his left hand. His right hand was badly blistered, thanks to his fight with Medusa. It was fine. He was a bold adventurer, and who needed use of their dominant hand anyway?

The ground was flat and littered with small animal bones. Mark passed his light over these curiously; most of them seemed to be from bats. Sending his beam across the ceiling, he noticed bunches of the brown fuzzy animals all sleeping huddled together. What kind were they? He made up his mind to look up the species as soon as he had internet again.

Proceeding deeper into the darkness, he caught sight of several larger animal skeletons on the floor. The nearest appeared to be from some kind of dog or a fox. Mark stooped down beside it for a closer look.

The skeleton was complete, clean, and intact. It took all of Mark's self-control not to pick it up to take home. Where would he pack it? The saddle bag he slashed was being held together with string. Besides, he had to stay focused on his mission.

He tore himself away, taking a sweeping look at the other skeletons lying across the floor. Most of them were like the fox, perfectly intact without any gnaw marks.

Odd, why would scavengers ignore the corpses of all these animals? And why were they all in exactly the same state of decomposition? None had any flesh or hair, they were just perfectly bleached, naked bone. Maybe all the creatures had been killed in the same incident? But what killed them?

Mark pulled himself from his musings when he noticed a white glow coming from the darkness ahead. It looked to him like fluorescent light. He proceeded toward it, stepping carefully around the beautiful skeletons.

The light grew brighter and brighter until it completely enveloped him. He slammed his eyes shut as the whiteness stung them. Then he heard the delighted squeals of children.

Mark opened his eyes and blinked until they adjusted. He seemed to be standing in some kind of living room. Two small children zipped around the space in circles, leaping over furniture and crashing into walls. In the center of the room, a man was slumped on a beaten sofa, staring at a television.

Mark glanced over his shoulder. The yawning blackness of the cave still loomed behind him, but before him and to either side were the three interior walls of a house.

Was this some kind of a vision?

"Hello?" he called to the man on the sofa.

The man made no response and the children continued their rowdy games undistracted.

Mark squinted at the children. Why wouldn't they come into focus? He checked to make sure his glasses hadn't fallen off but they hadn't. He just couldn't see them clearly. It was impossible to tell how old they were, or even if they were boys or girls. It was like some kind of dream.

The man on the sofa was perfectly clear. Mark took a few steps toward him and jumped when he recognized himself. This Mark was ten years older, he had a vacant, exhausted look in his eyes. But his mustache was... absolutely perfect.

Mark always thought of his mustache as his one feature that could not be improved. However, this future version of himself proved him wrong. The mustache on that man seemed to boldly proclaim to all the earth that its wearer was an acclaimed intellectual who deserved a Nobel prize.

"Hello?" Mark tried again.

His older self and the children ignored him. Perhaps he was only meant to be an observer in this dream world. Yet, something strange happened as Mark continued observation. His head began to ache and somehow he knew that the pain was coming from his future self.

He found himself exhausted, frustrated, and wondering why those kids *always had to be so loud*. While enveloped in the emotions and thoughts of his older self, he remained outside him, watching and experiencing feelings of his own.

"Alright, outside!" his older self ordered as one of the children took a flying leap onto the chair in the corner. The kids ignored him.

"*Outside!*" future Mark repeated, leaping up from the sofa. This time the littles obeyed, scurrying from the room.

Older Mark sighed and flopped back down as a distant door slammed. Younger Mark looked toward the television to see what he was watching.

It was some sort of documentary. Mark knew the woman being interviewed. They called her Oli back in school. She was brilliant, second to no one. Well... no one except Mark Reid. When Mark left Wellingford she must have taken his place as star student.

He always knew she'd do well... and here she was, getting introduced on some documentary as Doctor Olivia Jackson. Young Mark only caught a snippet of the program, but it seemed like she was trying to convince the interviewer that the elongated skulls discovered in South America were not, in fact, aliens.

Young Mark grinned. Poor Oli, she probably only agreed to do this interview to please her funders. Well, talking to a bunch of conspiracy theorists about her passion was better than talking to no one about it at all.

Older Mark was thinking about how ridiculous the whole thing was, and how he'd really dodged a bullet when he left the field.

Younger Mark's gaze dropped. He still had enough emotional autonomy to recognize jealousy in his older self. Oli, his rival, was living her dream; and what was he doing? Career-wise, Young Mark wasn't sure. Probably still pulling weeds on Cedar Hill and then coming home to a herd of rowdy children.

Frustration, jealousy, and anger oozed from Elder Mark, and wrapped itself around the Younger's heart. At the very same moment, a thin tentacle slithered from the darkness of the cave behind him and wrapped itself around the younger's ankle.

A door slammed, causing Older Mark to look up. Rosaline stormed in, bringing a thick cloud of tension with her.

"Is everything alright, Ros?" Older Mark called.

"Perfect," her voice snapped back, before she disappeared around a corner into the kitchen.

Older Mark gritted his teeth. Clearly, things were not "perfect," so why didn't Rosaline just come and tell him about it? He still had a splitting headache from dealing with the children and the last thing he needed was an angry wife thrown into the mix.

His resentment swelled and spread. Younger Mark could feel it burning into him. He sympathized with his elder self. Angry Rosaline was difficult at the best of times and he could see how dealing with that for ten years would make his older self resentful.

A second tentacle slithered forward from the blackness and snaked its way up younger Mark's leg. Still, he was so enveloped in the potential future unfolding before him, he didn't notice.

"When I was your age," Rosaline's voice echoed through the walls. "Men did men's work and women did women's work."

Who was she talking to? One of the kids?

"Now, *women* do men's work and women do women's work and do you know what men do? *NOTHING!*" she snapped.

Older Mark rolled his eyes. Why did she always do this? Why didn't she just ask him for help? Well, until she was ready to come and talk to him like a mature adult, he wasn't going to do anything. Resentment, frustration, jealousy boiled inside Older Mark.

A third tentacle emerged from the darkness and slipped around Young Mark's middle. Then, with its victim still transfixed on the scene before him, the owner of the tentacles undulated silently forward.

A deep sadness pierced Young Mark as he looked at his bitter older self.

"Go and talk to her," he mumbled.

Older Mark made no response. His anger stewed, his resentment deepened. Rosaline was the reason he'd lost everything. *Rosaline* was always demanding things, always frustrating him, nothing he ever did was good enough for her.

Young Mark winced as he felt the emotions of his older self snowballing.

"Stop it," he cried to his future self. "It isn't like that. Go to her and make it right."

But his older self ignored him. For suddenly it seemed as if every minor discomfort in Older Mark's life was the result of something *Rosaline* did. He tore her to pieces in his mind, destroying her, destroying them as a couple.

Young Mark reached into his breast pocket and withdrew the photograph Brother Joseph provided. He drank in her smile, stewed in the memories of that beautiful day. Courage, curiosity, wit, beauty, an adventurous spirit... that's what he was fighting for now. Why wasn't his bitter, resentful older self willing to fight?

Young Mark looked up from the photograph and scowled at his elder self.

"Go and talk to her!" he shouted.

He was alarmed when his older self responded. Not physically, but telepathically, as if he had mistaken Younger Mark for a voice in his own mind.

I already have. A lot of good it did.

"Well, do it again!" Young Mark ordered. "Bloody hell, mate! You fought Medusa for this woman! And you're not even going to try patching things up?"

When his older self made no response, young Mark lunged forward only to find himself stuck tight. That's when he looked down and noticed the tentacles around his waist and ankles. He froze, swallowed, and slowly turned around.

A translucent gelatinous blob towered behind him in the dim light. It had a tentacle-like appendage hanging from its head that ended in a white glowing orb like that of an angler fish. Through the translucent flesh, Mark could see the corpses of various species of native wildlife.

The blob appeared to be digesting these one layer of flesh at a time. A deer floating in the middle was missing the top layer of skin. A raccoon up and toward the back of the thing only had a few muscles clinging onto its bones.

This... giant amoeba, or whatever it was, clearly fed by enveloping prey, digesting the flesh, and spitting out the bones. Mark looked down at the blackish tentacles around his middle and ankles. The bottom of the blob was starting to envelop his boots.

He drew his sword and hacked at the tentacle around his waist. The blob didn't show any signs of pain as the rubbery tentacle broke off. Mark started on the ones at his feet, but as he did so, the stump of the former tentacle elongated into a new limb and wrapped around him again.

Mark stabbed directly into the blob but it made absolutely no reaction at all. It just kept drawing him slowly closer to its body. A fourth tentacle sprang from the body and began snaking its way through the air, toward Mark's wrist.

"Don't even think about it!" Mark cried, slashing it off.

No sooner had he slashed that off, then another tentacle sprung out of the blob and caught his opposite hand. Mark tugged against it, but couldn't break free.

He couldn't kill it with a sword, and he wasn't strong enough to fight against it. What could kill a giant blob? His mind raced. Inside his backpack, he had several moisture control packets that were clearly labeled DO NOT EAT.

Maybe he could dry it out? Like putting salt on a slug?

He twisted around, trying to remove his backpack. He got the strap to slide off his free arm, but the other strap just slipped down over the blob's tentacle.

As he squirmed, trying to reach it, his mobile fell out of his pocket.

Mark watched as it sank into the gelatinous body. The charging port sparked as it touched the moist flesh. The blob jolted uncomfortably and Mark swore as a spark of electricity jumped from one of the tentacles onto his bare wrist.

So this thing's gelatinous body was apparently very conductive. Thank God Mark had dropped his phone and not the charging stick. He might have been electrocuted–

Suddenly, he had an idea. Trouble was, if he tried it while he was still attached to the blob, he'd fry himself.

He struggled for his backpack, dug out a couple of dry packets and threw them onto the body. They made a sizzling sound as they touched the flesh.

The creature roared. Mark furrowed his brow and regarded the thing with his mouth slightly open as he contemplated a critical question—how could a creature without lungs or a mouth roar?

As the thing began violently shaking him, he realized this question wasn't actually that critical. He hacked at the tentacle on his wrist, snapping it. Then, as quickly as possible, he took care of the one around his waist and ankles.

The dry packs weren't enough to do any serious harm, but they clearly burned the amoeba or whatever it was.

He stumbled away just as the tentacles began to reform. Then he snatched the charging stick out of his backpack. These things usually had numerous safeguards to prevent electrocution. He grabbed a rock and began denting the area around the ports.

A tentacle reached for him; he didn't have any more time. He threw the stick at the body and watched as it was absorbed into the gelatin.

Sparks jolted through the creature, lighting up the cave. The lightbulb on the top of it flickered as the thing roared in pain.

Then, the roaring ceased and the cave was silent, save for a sizzling sound.

Mark watched in some strange combination of horror and relief as the thing slowly melted into a puddle of sticky goo.

"Give a kiss! Daddy, give a kiss?" Mark heard from over his shoulder.

He turned sideways so he could see how his older self was faring without taking his eyes off the dead amoeba.

A tiny child toddled toward his older self. While he couldn't get a clear look at her face, he knew that she was a little girl. She was cuddling a big, stuffed... *was that a spider?* It definitely had a lot of legs. Five of the legs had socks on them, each in a different color. Apparently, dressing up this plush... thing... was a habit of the child's.

"Look at this!" the toddler said holding the spider out to older Mark. "Kiss a spider," she ordered cheerfully. "A spider need a nap. Give a kiss."

Older Mark looked down at the girl, then broke into a weary smile. Then he took the spider and kissed it.

"Daddy kiss a spider," the little girl chatted happily. "Aw! A daddy kiss a spider."

Then the little girl raised up her arms toward him. "Up!" she demanded.

Older Mark's frustration still hung in the room, but now there was something else there with it—warmth, affection, love. He lifted the little girl onto the sofa.

While younger Mark couldn't see her face, he could see the dark curls that bounced all over her head. She was a little Rosaline, and he adored her. That love hadn't changed in his elder self.

"Why don't you watch television, sweetheart," his older self said as he changed the channel. "I've got to go talk to your mum."

The amoeba's light went out just as Elder Mark was standing up. With it, the vision vanished and Mark was left alone in darkness.

Mark was terrified to move lest he accidentally step in a puddle of electric goo. His torchlight seemed so dim after standing in the white light of the amoeba monster. Mark knew the battery in his light wouldn't last forever, he had to do something. *But what?*

If this was the final trial, where was the ring?

He passed his light over the melting blob and spotted something. A tiny wooden chest floating right in the middle of the charged gelatin. *Lovely.*

Slowly, carefully, watching his every step, he made his way around the remains of the blob and back out of the cave. A few moments later, he returned with the longest, straightest, stick he could carry.

The process of nudging the little chest out of the goo was long and tedious. Especially, because it kept getting lodged in more solid lumps of the thing's jelly-like flesh. The process became easier as the creature continued to melt.

Mark finally got his hands on the chest, only to discover it locked tight. At this point, his patience had long expired, so instead of looking for a key, he decided to stomp the wooden box to oblivion.

As it splintered open, something sparkled in the debris. Mark withdrew the item from the broken mess, a small galaxy of red stars bursting forth across the dark cave walls. Even in the dim light, Mark was raptured with the ring's beauty.

Desperate for a better look, he hurried it out into the sunlight and sat down on a rock to drink in the details. The silver setting was intricately woven with vine and floral designs hardly visible to the naked eye. The longer he looked, the more microscopic details he noticed. This was fairy work if he ever saw it.

Of course, the stone in the center was its crowning glory. The ruby was shaped with thousands of minuscule angles so that from the top, it looked like a rose. Tilted slightly, the angles made the petals of the "rose" seem more like spiraling flames. Deep crimson, vivid scarlet, and even a warm gold were all woven seamlessly together in that perfect stone.

Mark became almost drunk with joy at the thought of giving this to Rosaline. No ring like it existed anywhere in the world, and maybe none ever would. Brother Joseph had said that the ring's beauty would make all the hardship seem worth it. He was not exaggerating.

"Ah! There you are, Mark!" came a familiar voice.

Mark looked up to see the old monk himself strolling out of the cave.

"I see you got the resentment blob," the old monk continued. "Impressive, what you did to it."

Mark stood up. "The resentment blob?"

"Extremely dangerous," Brother Joseph continued. "It gets you fixated on grievances and then eats you alive."

A hundred questions flooded Mark's mind, but the one he managed to ask was:

"How does it roar without lungs?"

"It came from your subconscious," the old monk shrugged. "You tell me."

While Mark was pondering this, the monk patted Artemis's nose.

"In any case," he said. "I've got to get the two of you back now. I've only hired Artemis for a couple of days and Mr. Ariti will have my head if I don't return her on time."

Mark stiffened. "She's a real horse?"

Brother Joseph looked confused. "Why wouldn't she be?"

"But–but–she just stood there, with Medusa and the bomb and–"

"She's a tourist horse," Brother Joseph replied. "Nothing spooks her. Makes her perfect for beginners! Not to mention the fact that she's been up and down this trail so many times, she doesn't need any guidance at all anymore."

"Yeah, but–" Mark spluttered. "Medusa!"

"Exactly!" Brother Joseph answered. "No man who's fought Medusa has any reason to fear horses. Now, give her a carrot, Mark and tell her she's a good girl."

Mark did so jerking only slightly at the feel of the horse's velvety lips on his palm.

Conclusion

Mark wanted to go home and get showered and changed before going to see Rosaline. However, Brother Joseph suggested he take the ring to her immediately.

"She'll want you to present her with the ring while you're still covered in the blood of the monsters you killed to get it!" Brother Joseph insisted.

"This isn't really blood," Mark commented. "This is more like... blackish... goo."

"Perfect," the monk exclaimed. "It makes you look tough!"

Without waiting for Mark's response, he magically transported Mark and Artemis to the dirt road that led to Rosaline's stables. Mark mounted his horse and continued on the road until he spotted Rosaline outside the barn.

"Mark?" she asked, turning around. She froze when she saw him sitting on horseback, and then regarded him with a furrowed brow.

He had to be an uncanny sight, sitting there, covered in goo, his right hand bandaged, a sword at his hip.

Mark suddenly pictured himself boldly dismounting, then swooping to his knees before his princess. However, when he tried it, his foot caught in the stirrup and ended up in a crumpled heap with a couple more scrapes added to his collection.

"Mark, what happened to you?" Rosaline asked, as she helped him to his feet.

"Well, um, remember that story Brother Joseph told us about the Fire Stone?"

Rosaline nodded.

Mark fumbled in his pocket for a moment before holding it up for Rosaline to see.

Her jaw dropped. Silently, she took it and began drinking in the details.

"It's really it, yes?" she breathed. She was saying it more to herself than to Mark. The stone's authenticity was undeniable to anyone who got a good look at it. No human jeweler could produce a piece so intricate.

"You, you did the three trials and everything?" she said looking back up at him in disbelief.

Mark replied by telling her the entire story. Everything from the day he told Brother Joseph of his concern, to the day the monk made him aware of the quest. Then he told her all about Lady Eadburg's ghost, and Medusa, and the flesh-eating blob thing.

"In any case," Mark finished. "I wanted to give this to you because... I wanted you to know that, when you need me to fight for you, I will. You're worth that to me, Rosaline."

Rosaline grinned, blushed, and bit her lip as she looked down at the Fire Stone.

Mark's heart hammered in his chest as he waited for her to say something.

At last she said, "Go take a shower, Mark."

Mark raised an eyebrow.

"Because I *really* want to hug you and kiss you right now," Rosaline explained. "But not when you're covered in... bits of amoeba..."

Mark grinned and turned scarlet. "Yeah, yeah, I probably should."

They were both blushing and giggling now like embarrassed children.

"Oh, and Mark," Rosaline added.

She placed the ring back in his hand. "You are ruining the custom."

"I don't understand."

"I've seen a lot of films now, Mark," Rosaline asserted. "So I know the modern custom. You cannot give a woman a ring unless you first dress like a penguin, take her to a restaurant, genuflect, and ask for marriage."

Mark burst out laughing. "Well, yeah, usually, but I wasn't sure you were ready for that so I–"

"You can always ask, Mark," Rosaline smiled. "If I am not ready, I'll say no."

"Right," Mark grinned. "But the thing is, if you want to go by the custom, you only *get* the ring if you say yes."

Rosaline was chomping down on her lip, trying to prevent a torrent of giggles from escaping.

"Go home, Mark," she finally managed. "And do not return to me until you are in penguin costume."

"Is a pigeon alright?" Mark asked. "I've only got a gray suit."

"It is a poor man's bird," Rosaline sighed. "But it will do."

Mark was a little nervous as he entered the restaurant with Rosaline on his arm. He shouldn't have been, after all he'd known for some time that they were going to get married eventually. All they were really about to do was make their engagement official.

As they waited for their table, Mark found his mind wandering back to the vision he had in the cave of the resentment blob. The frustration, exhaustion, jealousy... was that what he was signing up for? That vision was created by a monster, was it even real? Was he seeing the future or just some strange dream?

He put his hand in his pocket and fiddled with the Fire Stone.

"What is that?" Rosaline suddenly blurted.

Her words snapped him from his thoughts. There was a little gift shop by the entrance of the restaurant. Rosaline was looking at a plush animal on a shelf near the door. At the sight of it, Mark froze.

"It looks like an octopus and a spider made love and God punished them with an unholy demon child," Rosaline commented.

"I need to get that," Mark stated.

Rosaline raised her eyebrows. "Are you alright, Mark?"

"Wait here," he said.

After a few moments, he emerged with the plush abomination and gave it to Rosaline.

"Is it the modern custom to give this to a woman you *don't* want to marry?" Rosaline teased.

"On the contrary," Mark smirked. "It makes me want to marry you more."

"You're mental," Rosaline laughed.

"Someday that... whatever it is... is going to be very special to someone important to us," Mark insisted. "Trust me on that."

It was a funny thing that a strange purple polka-dotted, spider-octopus hybrid plush would wipe fear of marriage from Mark's mind. However, when he saw it, with his fingers still fiddling with the Fire Stone in his pocket, several things fell into place in his heart.

Brother Joseph had said that seeing the fire stone's beauty would make all the struggle to find it worthwhile. He wasn't lying. When Mark glimpsed his future, he saw struggle, he saw frustration. It wasn't until after he'd killed the thing, that he saw a tiny glimpse of beauty—a sweet little girl who looked like Rosaline and wasn't afraid of kissing spiders.

Perhaps that weird plush was the universe's way of telling Mark that the beauty he had witnessed was like that of the Fire Stone. It made the fight worthwhile.

Acknowledgments

Because this is such a short book, I challenged Cecilia Lawrence to make me a cover in half the usual time. Can you tell? *Of course, you can't.* Cecilia is too good for that. Someday, I am going to reduce her timeline to five minutes just to see if she can throw together the *Mona Lisa* real quick.

Thank you, Grace Woods, for your interior illustrations. All of them made me smile, though Mark fighting Medusa in selfie mode nearly killed me.

Thank you, Helen for proofreading and thank you to everyone who beta read this book and gave me feedback.

Lastly, I want to thank the internet for introducing me to the word "novelette." If it wasn't for that vast wealth of questionable information, I might have continued telling everyone this was a "very, very, very short book."

Milton Keynes UK
Ingram Content Group UK Ltd.
UKHW022201290524
443431UK00013B/391